Licensed exclusively to Top That Publishing Ltd
Tide Mill Way, Woodbridge, Suffolk, IP12 1AP, UK
www.topthatpublishing.com
Copyright © Emma Levey 2014
All rights reserved
4 6 8 9 7 5
Printed and bound in China

Written and illustrated by Emma Levey

ISBN 978-1-78244-478-7

A catalogue record for this book is available from the British Library

'For Mam and Dad'

Hattie Peck

Written and illustrated
by Emma Levey

Hattie Peck had only ever laid one egg,
and it had never hatched.

Poor Hattie, she simply loved eggs.

They were all she thought about, and all she dreamed about.

Eggs, eggs, EGGS!

No egg was too

BIG.

No egg was too

small.

Hattie Peck loved them all.

But all she wanted was an egg of her own.

All this thinking and
dreaming about eggs made
Hattie Peck very sad.

But then she had a thought!
If she couldn't lay an egg,
she'd find one. In fact,
she'd find lots!

She plucked herself up and
decided to venture way
beyond her coop ...

… to embark on a journey in search of all the abandoned eggs.

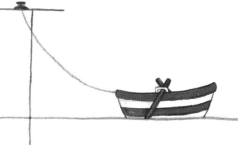

Hattie would rescue them,
and hatch every last one!

So off she went,
in search of the eggs.

Clucking and puffing,
she rowed for days on end across stormy seas.
Hattie battled weather like you've never seen.

She dived to the deepest depths of vast oceans.

If there was just one forgotten egg she could save ...

... she would find it!

Hattie Peck trekked through villages,

and clambered over rooftops ...

... gently guiding
precious little eggs
down the gutters
so as not to
crack them.

Plink!

Plop!

Hattie Peck soared over gigantic cities.

The mere thought of heights made Hattie shudder,
but she would do anything in search of her treasured eggs.

She hauled her plump little body up mountains.

towering far above the clouds ...

... and trudged through gloomy dark caves, deep down below the ground.

She battled
blazing fires …

blustery winds …

pouring rain ...

... and heavy snow.
All to find

eggs,

eggs,

EGGS!

And find them she did!

Hattie Peck decided it was
time to return with her
colossal clutch to her coop.
'What a tremendous task!'
Hattie thought.

As was sitting on them!

But Hattie Peck
didn't mind. She was
happy.

Days and even weeks went by, until finally ...

CRACK! SCRATCH! TAP!
The hatching had begun, and when it was done ...

Oh look!

Hattie Peck made the

perfect little mum!